Sparkleton
The Weirdest Wish

READ MORE SPARKLETON BOOKS!

1

2

3

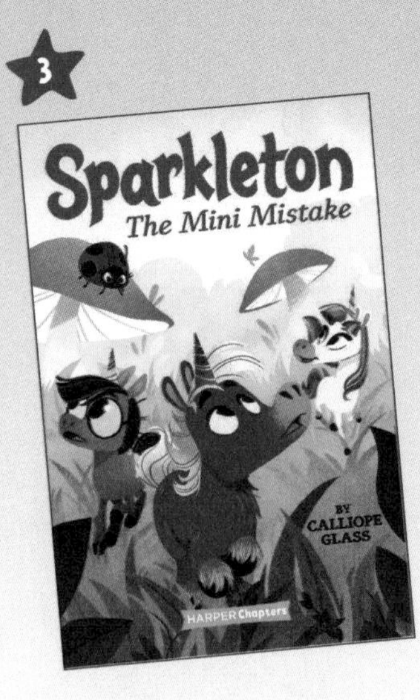

4

HARPER Chapters

Sparkleton

The Weirdest Wish

BY CALLIOPE GLASS

ILLUSTRATED BY
HOLLIE MENGERT

HARPER
An Imprint of HarperCollins*Publishers*

To Skeeter,

the first horse I ever loved.

Sparkleton #4: The Weirdest Wish
 For information address HarperCollins Children's Books, a division of HarperCollins Publishers, 195 Broadway, New York, NY 10007.
www.harperchapters.com
Library of Congress Control Number: 2020943979
ISBN 978-0-06-294801-4 — ISBN 978-0-06-294800-7 (pbk.)
The artist used Photoshop to create the digital illustrations for this book.
Typography by Andrea Vandergrift
21 22 23 24 25 EP 10 9 8 7 6 5 4 3 2 1
❖
First Edition

TABLE OF CONTENTS

1 Time for Winter!

It was the morning of the winter solstice. It was the shortest day of the year . . . and the best day of the year. Today at noon, the unicorns would slide on the ice and romp in the snow at the Winter Carnival!

"Time for winter!" Sparkleton yelled the moment he woke up. He jumped out of his bed of dry grass. He galloped to the edge of the glen where his family slept.

Then he sprang into the air so he could dive into the fluffy solstice snow!

CRASH!

Sparkleton dove all right. But he dove right onto the hard, bare ground. *Ouch!*

Where was the snow?!

If there was no snow this solstice, then—

"They're going to have to cancel the carnival," a gloomy voice announced behind him.

SPARKLETON

Can't wait to get wish-granting magic

Purple

Shaggy

Has a sore nose from his fall!

Sparkleton turned around. His best friends, Gabe and Willow, were standing there!

Gabe pawed the ground sadly.

"Snow can't fall when it's this warm outside," Gabe said.

Sparkleton sniffed the air and flicked his ears. Actually, now that they mentioned it . . .

"Wow," said Sparkleton. "It feels like spring. It even *smells* like spring. But the winter solstice is this afternoon. Britta was going to build a snow castle for the carnival luncheon and everything!"

Sparkleton stamped his hoof. If only he had wish-granting powers . . . then one of his friends could wish for snow and Sparkleton could grant their wish.

But Sparkleton hadn't gotten his magic yet. He was so, so tired of waiting!

"Don't worry. I've got a plan," Willow said. She lowered her voice. "Let's ask Zuzu, Britta, and Rosie to use the Pixie Cap to make it snow," she whispered.

Sparkleton pranced. "That's a *great* idea, Willow!" He could always count on her for dangerous solutions to minor problems!

The Pixie Cap was a magic hat that granted just one wish. Zuzu, Britta, and Rosie had won the cap at this year's talent show, but they hadn't used it yet!

Sparkleton, Gabe, and Willow found their friends moping next to Shimmer Lake. Zuzu was dipping her hoof in the water. Britta was staring at the only cloud in the sky. Rosie was holding the Pixie Cap.

BRITTA

Can't wait to build that snow fort for the WINTER CARNIVAL, which is TODAY AT NOON, except it hasn't SNOWED AT ALL

"The Pixie Cap," Sparkleton said in a slow, hushed voice. He couldn't take his eyes off it.

"We were going to use the Pixie Cap to wish for snow," Britta told him. "But then—"

"We thought maybe we shouldn't," Zuzu added.

What? thought Sparkleton. He didn't understand. *Why not wish for snow?*

"Because you all want to use it, but only one of you can?" Willow asked.

"No," Rosie said. "Because *none* of us want to use it."

2

This Is Not Good

Sparkleton just stared at his classmates.

"You see," Zuzu added, "we've *heard things* about the Pixie Cap."

"Bad things?" Willow asked eagerly. Willow loved trouble.

"We heard that the Pixie Cap is a lot of work," Rosie explained.

"Like, a *lot*," Britta said.

Suddenly, Sparkleton saw his chance. If his

friends didn't want to use the cap, *he* could use it! He could wish for wish-granting powers! He'd get his magic, wish for snow, and be the hero who saved the Winter Carnival!

He stepped up. "Maybe *I*—" he started.

"Okay!" Zuzu cried.

"Take it!" Britta said.

"It's all yours!" Rosie added. She dropped the cap on the ground, pushed it toward Sparkleton, then backed away.

“Well, this seems like a terrible idea,” Willow said cheerfully. “Put it on, Sparkleton!”

“This is not good,” Gabe muttered, but Sparkleton ignored him. Gabe worried about *everything.*

Sparkleton was so excited that his mane stood on end. The cap granted one wish, and

that was all he needed.

Sparkleton stared at the Pixie Cap. His heart was beating so hard he could feel it in the tips of his ears and the bottoms of his hooves.

Stars, he thought, *I hope this works.*

He lowered his head and moved it toward the Pixie Cap. He held his breath.

"Wait!" Gabe cried.

"What?!" snapped Sparkleton.

"Don't put it on," Gabe begged. "Even *Zuzu* thinks it's a bad idea."

"What's so bad about making one little wish?" Sparkleton asked impatiently. He glared at Gabe. "You never want me to have any fun."

Gabe looked at Rosie.

"First of all . . ." said Rosie impatiently, "everybody knows you shouldn't make wishes about the weather. Weather is too complicated! You wish for a rainbow in the meadow and

you end up with a typhoon in the dell. But also," she went on, "we don't know *anything* about the cap. For all we know, it was made by *goblins.*"

Sparkleton sighed. Everyone agreed goblins were bad news. But no one had ever seen a goblin. No one was even sure they were real.

Well, except for Willow. She was obsessed with goblin lore.

Sparkleton rolled his eyes. "Even if goblins made the Pixie Cap . . ." he said, "so what? Who cares? As long as it can grant a wish!"

"No one is sure what goblins can do . . ." Willow said dreamily.

"You know what *I* can do?" asked Britta. "I can build a snow castle—if we ever get some snow!"

"That's right!" said Sparkleton. He stood up tall. "I am not afraid of goblin magic! I'm brave! I'm going to save the day!"

"And get some wish-granting magic for yourself," Gabe pointed out.

"Sure," Sparkleton agreed. "Everybody wins!"

Before Gabe could stop him again, Sparkleton slid into the Pixie Cap.

It was a perfect fit!

You've already read 1,025 words. You must LOVE reading as much as Willow LOVES goblins!

3

I Hardly Ever *Stop* Talking!

As it settled on his head, Sparkleton could feel the power of the cap.

He was ready to make his wish!

But before he could open his mouth to speak, Willow started shouting from the other side of the meadow.

"Hey, everyone!" Willow called. "Come quick!"

All the unicorns except Sparkleton rushed

over to see what was going on.

Hey, thought Sparkleton. *What about me? I'm about to save the day!*

Now he was all alone with the cap.

"Fine," Sparkleton said to himself. "So . . . how do I even do this?"

Good question! a voice said. Sparkleton looked around, but there was nobody there.

How are you, young unicorn? the voice added. Sparkleton jumped straight into the air. The voice was coming from inside his head!

"How—?" he said. "What—?"

It's me, the voice said. *The Pixie Cap!*

"You *talk*?" Sparkleton asked.

I sure do! the Pixie Cap said. *In fact, I hardly ever* stop *talking! That's the thing about being a magical hat! It's hard to talk without a mouth. So you have to wait for some young unicorn to pop you onto his head. That way you can speak directly into his mind, using hat magic. And then . . . chatter city! Yammer, yammer, yammer. I love talking!*

"I want to make a wish," Sparkleton broke in.

Oh no, the hat said. *I wouldn't recommend that at all. Terrible idea. Don't do it.*

"Wait," Sparkleton said. "What?!"

You heard me! the hat said. *Hard not to, when I'm yelling directly into your brain. In fact, good luck tuning me out.*

YAMMER
YAMMER
YAMMER

Sparkleton tried again. “Maybe you don’t understand,” he told the cap. “I’m going to use you to wish for wish-granting powers, see? And then I’ll have wish-granting magic forever and ever! And I can use my magic to save the Winter Carnival somehow! I’ll be a hero!” He did a little happy dance.

He waited for the hat to tell him how smart he was.

Nope, said the hat.

"Nope?!" said Sparkleton. "What do you *mean*, 'nope'?"

Against the rules, said the hat.

"There are *rules*?" Sparkleton asked. He was starting to get annoyed.

Oh, so many rules, the cap said. *And rule number 13 is: No wishing for more wishes.*

This was bad news. Sparkleton took off at a gallop and caught up to Gabe.

"Gabe," Sparkleton said, nudging his friend with his shoulder. "I need a favor." He put on a winning smile. "How about you wear the cap instead? Then *you* can wish for *me* to have wish-granting magic! Easy-peasy." He held out his hoof to shake on it. Gabe looked nervous.

Then the hat had to pipe up. *That won't work either*, it said. *It's also against the rules. Rule number 215. Good rule. Always liked that rule.*

Say, kid, you want to hear a really long, boring story?

"Ugh!" Sparkleton cried. "These rules are so dumb!"

4 It's *Always* Goblins!

"Wait," Gabe said as they trotted after Willow and their other friends. "Are you . . . *talking* to the hat?"

"Yeah," Sparkleton said. "Though it's kind of hard to get a word in edgewise. It's got all these rules."

Suddenly, he had a great idea.

"What if I wished for the rules to be different?" Sparkleton asked the hat.

Rule number 78 says no to that, the hat replied. *So, anyway, about that story . . .*

Ahead of them, Willow broke into a gallop, and the others followed.

"Wait, Willow, I need your help!" Sparkleton called. But she ignored him.

"Over here!" Willow called to Britta, Zuzu, and Rosie. "Look!"

She was leading them toward a tree.

"Is it . . . *blooming*?" Zuzu asked. "How did that happen?"

"I told you!" Willow said, leaping excitedly. "Something strange is going on. It's spring in winter!"

Sparkleton trotted over to them.

"Something strange is going on all right," he told Willow. "I can't get the Pixie Cap to grant my wish!" He was sure Willow would know what to do.

But Rosie was showing her something. "Is that a robin?" she said, pointing to a bird with a bright red belly. "In the middle of winter?"

"*Goblin magic*," Willow said breathlessly. She stomped her hoofs in a unicorn clap. "There's no telling what it'll do next!"

Sparkleton looked around. "Wait. There's a goblin? Where? Did I miss something?"

Britta, Zuzu, Rosie, and Willow all talked at the same time.

Strange things are happening . . .
The trees are blooming . . .
The sky is too blue . . .
Shimmer Lake feels warm, not cold . . .

"And that's not all!" Willow announced dramatically. "See, I have an *idea*."

Her eyes were wide and her nostrils were quivering. Sparkleton had never seen her look so excited.

"About the Pixie Cap?" Gabe asked.

"About my wish?" Sparkleton asked. Had Willow figured out a way for him to get magic without using the cap at all?

"No!" Willow said. She had a wild look in her eyes. "About the *goblin*."

"Oh, here we go again," said Gabe.

"Well, you know my motto," Willow said.

Willow had a lot of mottos. It wasn't always easy to guess which one she meant. "'It isn't mischief if you don't get caught'?" Sparkleton tried.

"'There's no such thing as a dangerously bad idea'?" Rosie asked.

Willow shook her head. “I mean this one: It’s *always* goblins!”

Sparkleton hated that motto.

Willow lowered her voice, and the other unicorns gathered around. “Friends,” she said, “there’s a goblin lost in Shimmer Lake, I just *know* it.”

Gabe frowned. “What does that have to do with all this weird stuff going on?”

"Well, for one thing," Willow said, "goblins panic. They don't like leaving home. This one must be very scared. So it's making magic all over the place. It can't even stop itself!"

Britta added, "And maybe its magic has stopped the snow?"

"Which would make sense, because goblins hate the cold!" Willow added.

Rosie stomped her foot. “Well, we have to find it and send it home before it ruins the Winter Carnival!”

“That only gives us three hours!” cried Zuzu.

“We have to find it *now*!” Willow agreed. “Let’s go!”

Oh, GLITTER! How do you think we’ll solve this problem?

5

I'm Allergic to Rules

The four of them trotted away, chattering. Gabe just shook his head.

"How in glitter does Willow just *know* there's a goblin on the loose?" Gabe said.

Sparkleton snorted. "How in glitter does she think she's going to find it?"

"And what happens if she does?" Gabe asked.

Sparkleton's eyes grew wide.

If there really was a goblin—and it was stopping the snow—then Willow's plan would save the Winter Carnival!

That was sparkletastic, right? Sure, of course it was! After all, Sparkleton wanted to hide in Britta's snow castle. He wanted to make a pile of snowballs!

But . . . he also wanted to make a wish.

And he *also* wanted to save the day. But he couldn't save the day if Willow did it first.

Sparkleton turned to Gabe. "I have to save

the carnival before Willow does," he said. "I have to beat her to it."

Gabe shook his head gloomily. "Have either of us ever beaten Willow . . . at anything?" he asked.

"Good point," Sparkleton had to admit. "But there's always a first time! I just need to make one little wish and, *poof* . . . problem solved! The carnival will be on!"

"What about the goblin?" Gabe asked doubtfully.

"Goblin shmoblin," said Sparkleton. "I've got bigger problems. Like getting around all these rules. How many rules *are* there, anyway?" Sparkleton asked the Pixie Cap nervously.

There are 843 rules for using a Pixie Cap, the hat replied cheerfully.

AH-CHOO! Sparkleton sneezed.

"Sorry," he said. "I'm allergic to rules."

Well, that's too bad for you, the cap said. *Because now I'm going to tell you all 843 of them. Ready?*

"Not exactly," Sparkleton said.

Great! the Pixie Cap said. *Listen closely, because you really need to remember these.*

Rule number 1: No wishes about dandelions.
Rule number 2: No wishes for anything sparkly, except on the first Tuesday of the month.
Rule number 3: No wishes on a full moon.
Rule number 4: Only wishes on days that end in "y."
Rule number 5: No wishes standing on your head.
Rule number 6 . . .

The cap droned on. Sparkleton could feel his eyes crossing.

"What's the cap telling you?" Gabe asked.

"Everything!" Sparkleton complained.

Rule number 121: All wishes must be said out loud. Rule number 122: No funny wishes. Rule number 123: No sad wishes. Rule number 124: A . . .

He couldn't take it for one more second!

6

I'm Ready to Make My Wish

"Okay," Sparkleton said to the cap. "I can't wish for wish-granting magic. But there has to be a way around that, right?"

Nope, said the cap. But Sparkleton ignored it. He had an *amazing* idea.

"I'm ready to make my wish," he said.

I'm ready when you are, the cap replied.

Sparkleton closed his eyes tight and made a new wish.

"I wish for all my dreams to come true," he said grandly. After all, his biggest dream was to have wish magic. But if he didn't *say* that, then the rule couldn't stop him. Right?

Suddenly, Gabe was by his side. "Even that dream where you turn into a sea horse?"

Sparkleton jumped. He waved his horn in the air, erasing the idea. The last thing he wanted was to turn into a sea horse!

"No, no. Forget I said that," he told the Pixie Cap. "I'll try again. I wish to . . . follow in my family's footsteps." They all had wish-granting magic already.

Gabe tilted his head curiously. "You really want to be like Nella?"

Sparkleton shivered. He only wanted the same kind of magic as his bossy, annoying older sister, Nella. "No, that's not it," he told the cap. "Hang on."

Sparkleton tried again. And again. And again.

I wish . . . for a different way to get my wish.
Rule number 82.
I wish I could have two wishes.
Rule number 112.
I wish I could have all the wishes.
Rule number 43.
I wish I had my magic!
Rule number 15.
I wish I was in the snow castle **RIGHT NOW!**
Rule number 77.

"Argh!" Sparkleton yelled. He stamped his hooves. He wished for so many things, and this stupid cap had a rule for every single one!

"Is everything okay?" said a voice. Sparkleton knew that voice. It was the voice of Twinkle, the nicest unicorn in Shimmer Lake.

Twinkle would never try to sneak around the rules. She was the opposite of sneaky. She was perfect. And perfectly annoying.

"Oh, I love your hat!" Twinkle exclaimed. "You have such style, Sparkleton!"

Sparkleton sighed. "Twinkle, if you could wish for anything, what would you wish for?"

"That's hard," Twinkle said. "I'd have to think about what would make the most unicorns happy."

Of course, Sparkleton thought. Always thinking of others. So annoying. "Thanks," he muttered. *I wish she would go away now*, he thought.

"Happy to help," Twinkle said with a friendly flick of her tail as she trotted off.

Which gave him a great idea.

7

We Need a Little Help

"We need a little help, and I know just where to go!" Sparkleton told Gabe. "Gramma Una will know what to do with the Pixie Cap."

Whee! the cap yelled into his brain as Sparkleton took off to find Gramma Una.

Sparkleton and Gabe galloped off toward Gramma Una's cave library. But on the way, they ran into Willow. She was leading a group of young unicorns, including Twinkle and Dale.

"Come help us catch the goblin!" Willow called to Sparkleton and Gabe. Sparkleton shrugged. Gramma Una would still be there later, and he was curious to see what Willow was up to. After all, he wanted to save the day before Willow. And that meant keeping an eye on the competition.

The foals all trotted along in a cluster, keeping an eye out as they went. Willow told everyone what to look for.

"Goblins are little," she announced. "They're

smaller than us, and they walk on two feet. They have long, thin noses, and their ears stick out on the sides."

Britta and Zuzu peered behind some trees.

Dale looked into a bed of straw.

Rosie dug through a pile of pine cones.

Twinkle sang, "Come out, come out, wherever you are!"

“This is silly!” Sparkleton muttered to Gabe. “There isn’t any goblin!”

“But what if there is?” Gabe asked, his eyes wide.

“Have you ever actually *seen* a goblin?” Rosie asked Willow.

“No,” Willow admitted. “Nobody has. But I know a lot about them.”

“Why is it even here?” Dale asked.

"I have a theory," Willow said. "See, goblins live in Sulfurania. That's their underground kingdom. It's way down there, and it's super hot. Goblins don't like to come up to the surface because it's too chilly for them under the open sky. Somehow this poor goblin got stuck up here! Now he's really cold, running around Shimmer Lake."

"That makes no sense," said Sparkleton.

"Didn't his magic make it too warm for snow?"

"Sure," said Willow. "But it's still too cold for a goblin. They swim in lava lakes for fun! He must be hiding someplace. But if he warms up, he'll come out. And then he'll find his way home!"

Willow craned her neck around. "Okay, so where's Nella?" she asked.

Nella? Willow was going to team up with his bossy older sister? Sparkleton couldn't believe his ears.

"Willow's going to wish for warm clothes for the goblin," Zuzu explained. "And Nella will grant her wishes!"

"We'll leave the clothes around Shimmer Lake so he can find them," Rosie added. "That way, he'll be warm enough to look for the way home. When his magic is gone, the snow will come. And we can have the Winter Carnival!"

Sparkleton shook his head sadly. "Now *Nella* is going to save the day?" he said.

Nella trotted over to the rest of the foals. "Ready?" she asked Willow.

"Ready," Willow said. "I wish for one goblin-size wooly hat."

Nella began the spell.

First, she stamped her front hooves: left, then right.

Then she lowered her nose to the ground and snorted three times.

Finally, she traced a figure eight in the air with the tip of her horn. It began to glow. Nella looked deep into Willow's eyes. Willow stared back.

"Thy wish is granted," Nella said. She tapped Willow on the nose with her horn. A warm, wooly cap appeared out of nowhere with a *POP*.

Sparkleton got the shivers just watching it. Oh, how he wanted wish-granting magic of his own!

You still have a wish, the Pixie Cap pointed out. *Well, technically. You just have to figure out one that doesn't break the rules. Good luck with that!*

You're more than halfway through! You're putting in so much EFFORT!

7

8

You're Stuck with Me . . .

Willow nosed the wooly hat gently.

"Oh, it's *perfect*!" Willow told Nella. She pranced happily. "He'll love it, I'm sure!"

"Let's do the next one!" Nella said.

So Willow wished for gloves . . .

POP!

She wished for a long, striped scarf . . .

POP!

She wished for boots . . .

POP!

She wished for socks, mittens, long johns, earmuffs, elbow warmers, and a big, fluffy coat for the goblin.

POP! POP! POP! POP! POP! POP!

When she was finally finished, the young unicorns whinnied happily and pranced around the pile of warm winter clothes. They were excited about their plan!

But Sparkleton had a plan of his own. There was still time for him to get his wish and maybe even save the carnival after all . . .

He found Gramma Una inside the wide, sheltered cave where she kept all her books. Their pages were fluttering as if they were in a spring breeze.

"Oh, Sparkleton!" Gramma Una said. "I see you've put on the Pixie Cap. Wonderful! How's it going so far?"

"Awful," Sparkleton admitted. "I just want to make my one wish and have some fun! But there are all these *rules*."

Gramma Una grinned. "There certainly are," she said. "The Pixie Cap is a bit of a puzzle, isn't it? You have to work hard to figure out how to use it. It really is a glitterrific educational tool."

Sparkleton groaned. "But I don't *want* to be educated," he said. "I want to go to the Winter Carnival!"

"I'm afraid you don't have a choice," said Gramma Una, smiling.

Then she added some extra bad news.

"There's another thing about Pixie Caps," she said. "Once they're on your head, they're stuck there. The only way to get rid of them is by making a wish. But it's very hard to find a wish you're allowed to make. You have to be patient and thoughtful."

Sparkleton felt a little weak in the knees.

Yep, she's right, the Pixie Cap told Sparkleton. *You're stuck with me and all my rules. Should we review some more of them? Oh, you'll love this one. Very relevant to our current situation . . .*

Sparkleton sighed. "Am I *really* going to love it?" he said.

No, of course not, said the cap. *I was using sarcasm.* It cleared its throat. *Rule number 487: No removing the cap before a wish has been granted.*

Sparkleton did not love rule number 487.

The cap went on. *Rule number 488: No wishes for earthworms. Rule number 489: No wishes for people who fart and then blame it on other people. Rule number 490: All wishes are permanent. No take-backs. Rule number 491: No boring wishes. Rule number 492 . . .*

480 . . .
mber 481 . . . Rule number 482 . . .
Rule number 483 . . . Rule number 484 . . .
Rule
486 . . . Rule number 487 . . . Rule number 488 . . .
number 489 . . . Rule
er 490 . . .
Rule numbe
Rule number 492 . .
umber 49
number 495 . . . Rule
Rule
98 . . .
. . . Rule number
Rule nu
ule number 500 . . .

But Sparkleton was still stuck on 487. "No way," he said stubbornly. "I don't believe it."

He lowered his head and scraped at the Pixie Cap with his front hoof. But it stayed put. Then Sparkleton plopped onto his haunches and batted at the cap with *both* front hooves. But that didn't work either.

Grinding it against a rock didn't work. Setting it on fire didn't work—and the fire singed Sparkleton's

mane. Coating it in honey and trying to get ants to eat it didn't work, *and* it made a huge mess.

Sparkleton flopped over in frustration.

"Now you know how I feel most of the time," Gabe said.

9 There *Is* No Bright Side!

The other unicorns had carried the pieces of cozy goblin-wear all over the place. They left the sky-blue hat on a tree stump in the fern glen. They draped the scarf over a blueberry bush by the cliff. The coat was left on the big rock in the meadow, and the mittens sat at the foot of the tallest tree in Shimmer Lake. But so far nothing had happened.

One by one, Sparkleton's friends flopped

down beside him, and soon Nella came, too.

"This is the worst," Zuzu said glumly. "Sparkleton has a cap stuck to his head. There's a homesick goblin loose in Shimmer Lake. And the Winter Carnival is supposed to start in an hour."

"I'll *never* get to build my snow castle," Britta said. She sniffled sadly.

"Look on the bright side," Twinkle said cheerfully. "There's *always* a bright side."

"Okay, so what's the bright side here?" Rosie asked.

Twinkle had to stop and think for a while. Then she perked up. "I know!" she said.

"Yes?" Rosie said.

"This is one hundred percent a total disaster," Twinkle said. "And that *never* happens. So if you think about it, that's kind of cool all by itself!"

Meanwhile, the Pixie Cap would not pipe down. *Rule number 823: No wishes by or about butterflies* . . . it said.

Willow nosed Sparkleton sympathetically. "Is there *anything* you can wish for?"

"I don't even know," Sparkleton said.

"Maybe I can help," Willow offered.

Sparkleton looked at Willow gratefully. Suddenly, it seemed sort of silly that he'd wanted to beat her. Who cared *who* saved the day, as long as the day got saved? And this was Willow—one of his best and oldest friends. He was on her side, and she was on his.

"Thank you," he said. "Can you just come up with some ideas for wishes? Eventually we'll probably get to a wish that isn't against the rules. And I can make it—and then at least I'll be free!"

"Okay," Willow said. She thought for a moment. "I wish this leaf was orange."

Forbidden by rule number 554: No wishes to turn things orange, the cap said.

Sparkleton shook his head. "Nope," he told Willow. "Try another one."

Willow wished to make a rock slightly bigger. She wished to create a very small breeze. She wished for a cupcake, and she wished for an apple. But all her wishes were forbidden by some rule or another.

"I wish that Pixie Cap was off your head," Willow tried.

Ha! the Pixie Cap said. *Nice try, but rule number 757 says—*

Sparkleton shook his head no for Willow's benefit.

"This is really frustrating," Willow said.

"Tell me about it!" said Sparkleton.

Tell you about it? said the cap. *How about I tell you the very last rule? Rule number 843: No wishing for more than 843 rules. That's it.*

The last rule. All done.

There was a moment of perfect silence.

At last! Sparkleton thought. Then the cap started gabbing again.

So now you know every single rule! the hat said to Sparkleton. *Can you figure out a wish that doesn't break the rules? Think hard! You'll need to be very patient—*

"What's happened now?" Willow asked curiously.

"It's telling me to be *patient*," Sparkleton said.

Gabe winced.

"Oh dear," Willow said.

Twinkle tilted her head. "What's so terrible about that?"

"Sparkleton hates being patient as much as Gabe hates being chipper," Rosie told her.

"*Look!*" Willow said, and everyone jumped. Willow pointed her horn toward a tree stump on the other side of the fern glen. "We left the goblin's hat on that stump," she said. Her voice was shaking. "And now it's *gone*!"

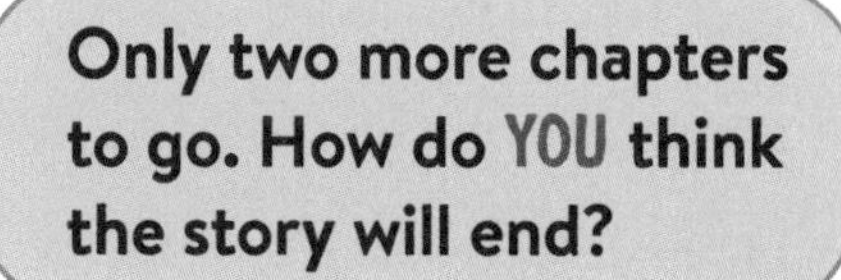

10
Sparkleton's *Thinking*

"Where did it go?" Twinkle asked.

"I think the goblin took it!" Willow said. She took off at a gallop. The unicorns all followed her until she skidded to a halt at the blueberry bush. "The scarf is gone, too!" Willow said.

The coat was gone from the rock in the meadow. The mittens were gone from the big tree.

The goblin was really real!

Sparkleton almost forgot about the Pixie Cap, he was so exci—

Did you figure out a wish yet? the cap demanded.

Sparkleton sighed.

"No," he said. He wasn't sure who to feel sorrier for. Himself, for being stuck with this cap on his head? Or the goblin, for being stuck in Shimmer Lake when all he wanted was to be safe at home?

"That poor goblin," Sparkleton said. If only he could grant the *goblin's* wish.

Wait.

Yyyyes? the cap asked. Sparkleton could have sworn it was smiling.

Sparkleton turned to Willow. "Willow," he said. "Are you sure the goblin *really* wants to go back home?"

Willow's eyes got very wide.

"I am," she said. "I bet he's wishing for it *right now*."

Sparkleton thought very hard. He thought about every single rule the hat had told him about. He thought about rule number 55 (No granting wishes to groundhogs on their birthdays) and rule number 163 (All wishes must be granted standing up). He thought for a long time.

"This is boring," Britta said. Zuzu had fallen asleep on her feet.

"Shhh," Gabe said. "Sparkleton's *thinking.*"

"Possibly for the first time ever," Nella quipped.

Sparkleton thought and thought. But he couldn't think of a single rule against wishing for a lost goblin to get back home.

Good job, the hat said. *Took you long enough.*

Sparkleton opened his eyes. "I'm ready," he told his friends.

Sparkleton closed his eyes and thought very hard about the goblin. Willow said goblins were about two feet high. She said their ears stuck out. And this goblin was wearing a sky-blue hat and a warm coat.

Sparkleton thought about a homesick goblin wearing a blue hat, wishing to go back to Sulfurania, deep beneath the surface of the earth.

"I wish you could go home," Sparkleton told the goblin, wherever it was.

11

It's *Cold* Again!

POOF.

A warm spark flew into the air from the tip of the Pixie Cap. Sparkleton watched it fizz up until it vanished against the blue sky. He shivered all over. The tips of his hooves tingled. *Something* had happened. Had he really granted the goblin's wish?

POP!

The Pixie Cap leapt off Sparkleton's head. It

sprouted two tiny legs and took off running down the beach.

So long! it said as it ran. Its "voice" inside Sparkleton's head got fainter the farther it went. *It's been real!*

The Pixie Cap vanished into the distance.

Sparkleton watched it go, shaking his head. What a weird day. What a weird hat. What a weird wish!

"Sparkleton's a hero!" Twinkle yelled. Sparkleton jumped a mile and whipped around.

"Come look!" Twinkle called. Twinkle, Gabe, and Willow were gathered on the other side of the big tree.

Sparkleton and the other young unicorns galloped over. Willow was nosing a pile of warm woolen winter clothes.

“You sent the goblin back home!” Britta said.

Nella bumped Sparkleton with her shoulder in a unicorn hug. “I can’t believe I’m saying this,” she said, “but . . . I’m proud of you, Sparkleton.”

“And you got rid of that horrible Pixie Cap,” Gabe said. “Good job. That thing was awful.”

“Sparkleton’s a hero!” Twinkle yelled again.

I am, thought Sparkleton.

Sparkleton blushed so hard even the tips of his ears turned pink. He *was* a hero! And now everyone knew it!

"Hooray for Sparkleton!" Rosie cried. And everyone whinnied as loud as they could.

Sparkleton pranced a little.

"Thanks, everyone," he said. "I know, I know, I'm really great. You should probably keep cheering for a long time."

Nella rolled her eyes.

But Zuzu said, "Okay! Hip hip—"

And everyone else yelled, "Hooray!"

This went on for a while, and Sparkleton loved every single minute of it. He loved being a hero. He loved having the Pixie Cap gone. He loved granting wishes. He loved—

"SNOW!"

The cry rang out through the crowd.

"Snow! It's snowing! Finally!"

A perfect snowflake landed on the tip of Sparkleton's nose. He stared at it in amazement.

Willow was staring at it, too, so their eyes met. "You really did it!" she said, nosing her friend. "Sparkleton, you saved that poor goblin with your one and only wish!"

Sparkleton beamed. "I did! But . . . I wouldn't have thought of it without you."

"It's *cold* again!" Dale exclaimed.

"Now that the goblin's gone, we can have the Winter Carnival!" Zuzu said.

"I'll get to make my snow castle!" Britta said.

"Another cheer for Sparkleton!" Rosie yelled. "Hip hip—"

"No, no," Sparkleton said. "It's too much, please. No more."

Everyone stared at him.

"I'm *kidding*!" Sparkleton said. "I saved the first day of winter! Hooray for me!"

"HOORAY!" all of Shimmer Lake yelled.

CONGRATULATIONS!

You've read **11** chapters,

87 pages,

and **5,660** words!

Hip hip, hooray! Feeling sparkletastic?

If you've read **ALL FOUR** Sparkleton books, you've read 23,342 words!

I **WISH** I had 23,342 wishes!

So anyway, what will you read **NEXT**?

UNICORN GAMES

THINK!

Try making up your own rules! With a friend, invent a game that uses one hat, a pair of dice, and ten blank index cards. What rules will you need to make sure the game is fun and easy to explain?

FEEL!

In this story, Sparkleton says he's allergic to rules. How do rules make you feel? Think about a rule you think is really helpful and one you'd like to get rid of. Why did you make the choices you made? Write about it in your journal or talk about it with a friend!

ACT!

Plan an imaginary winter carnival for your school! What games would you play? What snacks would you serve? What would you build in the snow?

Illustrated by Hollie Mengert

CALLIOPE GLASS is a writer and editor. She lives in New York City with two small humans and one big human, and a hardworking family of house spiders who are all named Gwen. There are no unicorns in her apartment, but they are always welcome.

Photo by Mike McCain

HOLLIE MENGERT is an illustrator and animator living in Los Angeles. She loves drawing animals, making people smile with her work, and spending time with her amazingly supportive family and friends.